SCELIDOSAURUS
(ske-LI-doh-SAW-rus)
TYRANNOSAURUS
(tie-RAN-oh-SAW-rus)
TRICERATOPS
(try-SER-a-tops)
STEGOSAURUS
(STEG-oh-SAW-rus)
PTERODACTYL
(TER-oh-DAC-til)
APATOSAURUS
(a-PAT-oh-SAW-rus)
ANCHISAURUS
(AN-ki-SAW-rus)

SCELIDOSAURUS
(ske-LI-doh-SAW-rus)
TYRANNOSAURUS
(tie-RAN-oh-SAW-rus)
TRICERATOPS
(try-SER-a-tops)
STEGOSAURUS
(STEG-oh-SAW-rus)
PTERODACTYL
(TER-oh-DAC-til)
APATOSAURUS
(a-PAT-oh-SAW-rus)
ANCHISAURUS
(AN-ki-SAW-rus)

Happy Birthday
to Ella, Teddy, Sophia
and Amelie – I.W.

Warwick Vincent Hutton
Born Friday 13 July 2007
7 pounds 8 ounces – A.R.

PUFFIN BOOKS
Published by the Penguin Group: London, New York, Australia, Canada, India, Ireland, New Zealand and South Africa
Penguin Books Ltd, Registered Offices: 80 Strand, London WC2R 0RL, England

puffinbooks.com

First published 2008
Published in this edition 2009
1 3 5 7 9 10 8 6 4 2

Made and printed in China

British Library Cataloguing in Publication Data
A CIP catalogue record for this book is available from the British Library

ISBN: 978–0–141–50051–5

Harry and the Dinosaurs have a Happy Birthday

Ian Whybrow · Adrian Reynolds

PUFFIN

There was wild excitement at Harry's house.
Harry and the dinosaurs were getting ready for a party.

"Let's go! Let's go! Let's go!" yelled Harry.
"Raaaah! Party!" cheered the dinosaurs.

But then Sam set off, leaving Harry behind.

"Why can't I go?" said Harry.

Sam said, "No way! I TOLD you! I'm going to a Girls Only party, and that's BIG girls too!"

Nan said to take no notice. "You come and help finish Mr Oakley's cherry pie," she said. "He's got his birthday tomorrow. He's going to be DEE-lighted if you take this over for him."

Apatosaurus said, "Raaah! We like making presents!"
"And birthdays! Raaaah!" said Anchisaurus.
"Raaaah! We can't have birthdays, can we, Harry?" said Stegosaurus.

"Yes you can," said Harry. "You can have your birthdays tomorrow, just like Mr Oakley."

On the way to Mr Oakley's the next day, Harry told Sam it was the dinosaurs' birthday. Sam said Harry was making it up just because he was jealous of other people going to parties.

"Raaaah!"

That was why Harry kept quiet about where she was treading.

When they got to the farm, Mr Oakley was in the pigsty feeding the piglets.

"Happy Birthday, Mr Oakley," said Harry. "Nan baked a cherry pie for you, and this card is from us."

“Harry made me stand in a cowpat,” grumbled Sam, and Harry said ha ha.

Mr Oakley was ever so pleased with his present, but he wanted to know why Harry and Sam were being nasty to each other.

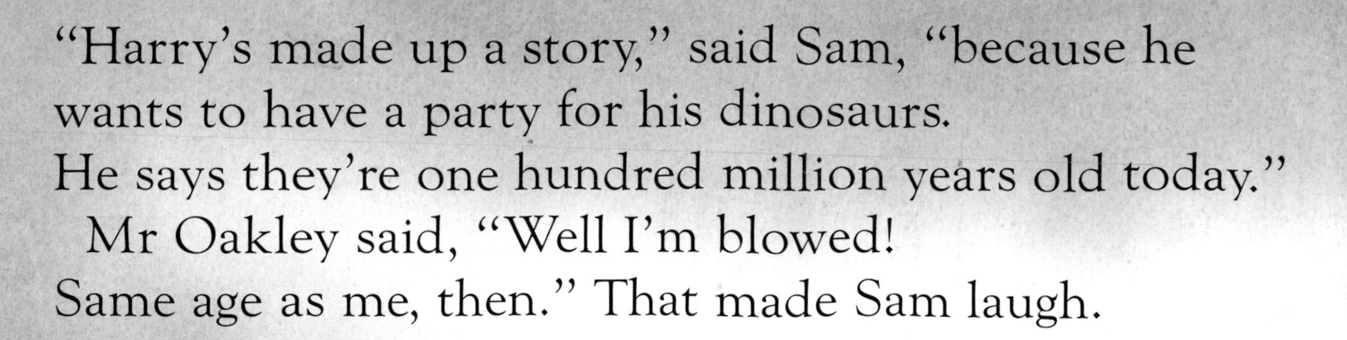

"Harry's made up a story," said Sam, "because he wants to have a party for his dinosaurs. He says they're one hundred million years old today."

Mr Oakley said, "Well I'm blowed! Same age as me, then." That made Sam laugh.

"Are you having a party, Mr Oakley?" asked Harry.

"I wish I was!" sighed Mr Oakley. "Only, I'm much too busy with my animals!"

When Harry got home, he told Nan he was sad about Mr Oakley not having time for a party.

"Cheer up!" she said. "Let's have a party for your dinosaurs, and Mr Oakley can share it with them."

Harry thought that was a great idea.

"We can make it a BIG surprise party!" he said.

There wasn't a lot of time to get ready, but Mum and Nan were quick workers. Harry invited Jack and Charlie. Even Sam joined in and made a jelly swamp . . .

. . . while Harry made some dinocakes!

"Raaaah! We like eating cakes," said Scelidosaurus.

"And we like ferns and ginkgo leaves!" said Tyrannosaurus. "Raaaah! They're prehistoric!"

"I like being a decoration," said Pterodactyl.

By four o'clock, everything was ready,
and everybody had their party outfits on.

Mum said SHHHH and phoned Mr Oakley.
She said could he please come over and help right
away, only the tap in the bath was stuck.

Then Nan led everyone into the garden to hide.

After a little while, the garden gate flew open . . .
and there was Mr Oakley with his toolbag.

"Raaah!" roared everybody. "Happy Birthday,
Mr Oakley, and Happy Birthday, dinosaurs!"

"Well I never, what a smashing surprise!"
said Mr Oakley. "Are we having games?"

Tyrannosaurus said, "Yes! Noisy ones! Rough ones!"
"Racing ones! Chasing ones!" said Anchisaurus.
"Jumpy ones! Scary ones!" said Triceratops.

So everyone did wheelbarrow racing round the hay bales.

They did hiding and pouncing and squirting and splashing.

Then they had a barbecue. There were veggie burgers for the herbivores and hot dogs for the carnivores.
Afterwards, there was jelly to jump in if you didn't want to eat it.

And at Happy-Birthday-to-You time, the dinosaurs stood nicely and held up the cake with candles for blowing out.

What a party!

Not one person cried and nobody wanted to go home because they said it was the best party ever.

“And which part of your birthday did you like best, my Pterodactyl?” said Harry at bedtime.

Pterodactyl said he liked the part when the dragon in the field breathed smoke on him.

Harry didn’t tell him that the dragon was a cow really and the smoke was her breath. After all, you only get ONE one-hundred-millionth birthday, so no point spoiling it.

ENDOSAURUS

SCELIDOSAURUS
(ske-LI-doh-SAW-rus)
TYRANNOSAURUS
(tie-RAN-oh-SAW-rus)
TRICERATOPS
(try-SER-a-tops)
STEGOSAURUS
(STEG-oh-SAW-rus)
PTERODACTYL
(TER-oh-DAC-til)
APATOSAURUS
(a-PAT-oh-SAW-rus)
ANCHISAURUS
(AN-ki-SAW-rus)

SCELIDOSAURUS
(ske-LI-doh-SAW-rus)
TYRANNOSAURUS
(tie-RAN-oh-SAW-rus)
TRICERATOPS
(try-SER-a-tops)
STEGOSAURUS
(STEG-oh-SAW-rus)
PTERODACTYL
(TER-oh-DAC-til)
APATOSAURUS
(a-PAT-oh-SAW-rus)
ANCHISAURUS
(AN-ki-SAW-rus)